Dear mouse f[...]
welcome to the [...]

Geronimo Stilton

The Editorial Staff of
The Rodent's Gazette

1. Linda Thinslice
2. Sweetie Cheesetriangle
3. Ratella Redfur
4. Soya Mousehao
5. Cheeslta de la Pampa
6. Mouseanna Mousetti
7. Yale Youngmouse
8. Toni Tinypaw
9. Tina Spicytail
10. Maximilian Mousemower
11. Valerie Vole
12. Trap Stilton
13. Branwen Musclemouse
14. Zeppola Zap
15. Merenguita Gingermouse
16. Ratsy O'Shea
17. Rodentrick Roundrat
18. Teddy von Muffler
19. Thea Stilton
20. Erronea Misprint
21. Pinky Pick
22. Ya-ya O'Cheddar
23. Mousella MacMouser
24. Kreamy O'Cheddar
25. Blasco Tabasco
26. Toffie Sugarsweet
27. Tylerat Truemouse
28. Larry Keys
29. Michael Mouse
30. Geronimo Stilton
31. Benjamin Stilton
32. Briette Finerat
33. Raclette Finerat

Geronimo Stilton
A learned and brainy
mouse; editor of
The Rodent's Gazette

Thea Stilton
Geronimo's sister and
special correspondent at
The Rodent's Gazette

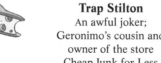

Trap Stilton
An awful joker;
Geronimo's cousin and
owner of the store
Cheap Junk for Less

Benjamin Stilton
A sweet and loving
nine-year-old mouse;
Geronimo's favorite
nephew

Geronimo Stilton

I'M TOO FOND OF MY FUR!

PUFFIN

PUFFIN BOOKS

Published by the Penguin Group
Penguin Books Ltd, 80 Strand, London WC2R 0RL, England
Penguin Group (USA) Inc., 375 Hudson Street, New York, New York 10014, USA
Penguin Group (Canada), 90 Eglinton Avenue East, Suite 700, Toronto, Ontario, Canada M4P 2Y3
(a division of Pearson Penguin Canada Inc.)
Penguin Ireland, 25 St Stephen's Green, Dublin 2, Ireland (a division of Penguin Books Ltd)
Penguin Group (Australia), 707 Collins Street, Melbourne, Victoria 3008, Australia
(a division of Pearson Australia Group Pty Ltd)
Penguin Books India Pvt Ltd, 11 Community Centre, Panchsheel Park, New Delhi – 110 017, India
Penguin Group (NZ), 67 Apollo Drive, Rosedale, Auckland 0632, New Zealand
(a division of Pearson New Zealand Ltd)
Penguin Books (South Africa) (Pty) Ltd, Block D, Rosebank Office Park, 181 Jan Smuts Avenue,
Parktown North, Gauteng 2193, South Africa

Penguin Books Ltd, Registered Offices: 80 Strand, London WC2R 0RL, England

www.puffinbooks.com
www.geronimostilton.com/uk

English-language edition first published in Great Britain by Scholastic Children's Books 2004
This edition published in Great Britain in Puffin Books 2012
003

Geronimo Stilton names, characters and related indicia are copyright, trademark and exclusive license
of Atlantyca S.p.A. All Rights Reserved.
The moral right of the author has been asserted

Text by Geronimo Stilton
Cover illustration by Andrew Farley and title lettering by Andy Horn
Illustrations by Lorenzo Chiavini and Roberto Ronchi
Graphics by Merenguita Gingermouse, Marina Bonanni and Beatrice Sciascia
Special thanks to Kathryn Cristaldi
Interior layout by Madalina Stefan Blanton

Text, illustrations and English translation copyright © 2000, 2004, Edizioni Piemme S.p.A., via Tiziano 32 - 20145
Milano – Italy

International Rights copyright © Atlantyca S.p.A., via Leopardi 8, 20123 Milano – Italy

Original title: *Ci tengo alla pelliccia, io!*
Based on an original idea by Elisabetta Dami

*Stilton is the name of a famous English cheese. It is a registered trademark of the
Stilton Cheesemakers' Association. For more information go to www.stiltoncheese.com*

Printed in Italy by Printer Trento S.r.l.

British Library Cataloguing in Publication Data
A CIP catalogue record for this book is available from the British Library

ISBN: 978-0-141-34121-7

MIX
Paper from
responsible sources
FSC™ C018179

I'm Too Young to Go Bald!

Let's see, it all began like this — it really did.

One evening, I was happily sprawled out on my couch, CHANGING CHANNELS on my TV, when a strange commercial caught my eye.

A female rodent with blonde fur was shouting **LIKE A MADMOUSE**. "Are you going bald? Has your fur lost its fluff?" Then she stuck her snout right up to the camera. "That's right, I'm talking to you, COUCH MOUSE!" she shrieked.

I jumped. Her beady little eyes seemed to be staring right at me!

"Now, do as I say and put your paw on your head," she ordered. *"I bet you have a bald patch. Am I right?"*

I gulped. With a shaking paw, I patted the top of my head. **Holey cheese!** My fur *did* seem to be getting a little thin on top! Could I really be losing my fur?

The mouse on TV kept squeaking at me. "Listen, **CHEDDARFACE**, you need to do something to strengthen your fur! If you don't, you're going to be as bald as a bowling ball down at Lucky Paw Lanes!"

She wound up her arm like a professional bowler rat. **"Striiike!"** she yelled, glaring at me.

I TURNED PALE...

I patted the top of my head.

Now I was really getting worried. I was too young to go bald. I was still in my prime. Yes, I think you could even call me a spring mouse. I still had a twitch in my tail, and my bones hadn't started creaking yet.

More hollering from the TV interrupted my thoughts. "Wake up, **NOODLEBRAIN**, because today is your lucky day! That's right. I have right here the cure for that **great-looking** bald spot! But you'd better order now, **you silly mouse**, or you'll be left with your tail between your legs!"

I grabbed a pen and paper to take notes.

The mouse on TV held up a helmet and a big bottle of green lotion. "This

MIRACLE
LOTION

HELMET

is a special kind of helmet that uses micro-macro-eeny-meany-miney-magnetic-waves. First you spread the MIRACLE LOTION all over your fur. Then you put the helmet over your head," she explained. "Keep the helmet on for at least two or three hours. The helmet SQUEEZES your head to WAKE UP those lazy hair roots. Got it?"

I nodded my head.

"Well, what are you waiting for, Baldy?!" the TV mouse squeaked at me. "Order now, *before they're all gone!*"

As if in a trance, I reached for the phone and dialed the number on the screen: **1-555-GROW-FUR**.

"Yes, I'd like to order one helmet," I began, patting my fur.

...I'd like to order one helmet...

The operator at the other end coughed. "I take it you must be tuned into our special supertelethon, **Baldies Unite!**" she said.

I choked. *I'm not bald yet!* I tried to say. But I had lost my squeak!

"Don't be embarrassed, Furless," the operator babbled on. "I'll send off your helmet right away! You want the MIRACLE LOTION, too, don't you? How MANY bottles? They are on special offer, you know."

I cleared my throat. "Um, well, I guess I could use two," I decided.

The operator lowered her voice and began to whisper CONFIDENTIALLY. "You sound like a very nice mouse," she began. "So I'm going to let you in on a *secret* . . . there are only a few bottles left!!!"

I **GASPED**. Were there really that many bald rodents scampering around out there?

"We've received so many calls," the operator continued KNOWINGLY. "The lotion is selling like hot cheese sticks at a winter carnival! I would

order a few more if I were you. *I think we're going to sell out!*"

I chewed my whiskers nervously. I couldn't wear my new helmet without the lotion. What if I ran out? I would be in big trouble then. I'd be one sorry, bald mouse. "I'd better order **3**, no **4**, no **5**, no make that **8**, or even **10**, yes, I'll take **10** . . . no, how about **12** bottles?" I stammered.

"Good choice," the operator murmured. "I'll put you down for twelve bottles. We'll deliver them right away.

Have your money ready!"

BALDIES UNITE!

Minutes later, the doorbell rang. *Ding...dong...*

It was a mouse with lots of thick, curly fur on his head. He was wearing Rollerblades and holding a package.

"Are you *Geronimo Stilton?*" he asked.

I nodded.

"Yes, that's me."

He *flashed* all of his thirty-two teeth. Then he stuck the

Delivery for Geronimo Stilton!!!!

package in my left paw and a bill in my right.

"Will that be cash or check?" he smiled.

"Um, check," I mumbled. I stared at the bill and turned white. I shrieked:

"I could buy a whole year's worth of cheese for this kind of money!"

QUICK as an alley cat, he snatched back the box. "Does this mean you're not paying? Did you change your mind?" he demanded.

"Um . . . well, it's just that it's a little *pricy*," I stammered.

The delivery mouse peered closely at my fur. "Wow, did you know you already have a bald spot?" He whipped out a mirror to show me.

BUT BEFORE I COULD CHECK, the delivery mouse stretched out his paw and yanked a tuft of fur from my ear.

"Just as I thought!" he cried. "Your fur is already falling out! Look at this clump!"

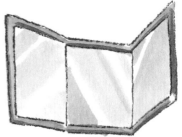

~ I stared down at my fur in his paw. My precious, fluffy brown fur! This was more **SERIOUS** than I'd thought.

"But does the helmet really work?" I asked, still not convinced.

The delivery mouse flashed his teeth again.

Then he **patted** his own head of thick, curly fur.

"I'm not just a delivery mouse," he grinned. "I'm also a client! I was as bald as a fresh ball of mozzarella before I started using this product!"

I paid the bill with a sigh of envy.

FRRRR . . . FRRRR . . .
ZZZZZ . . . ZZZZZ . . .

Back in my house, I smeared the MIRACLE LOTION onto my head. I put on the helmet and plugged it into the wall. Immediately, the helmet began MASSAGING my scalp.

Frrrrrrrrrr...frrrr...zzzz...

I plopped down in front of the TV. Right then, the phone rang.

"Hello?" I said.

I could just make out a voice. "I would like to speak with Geronimo Stilton, the editor of *The Rodent's Gazette*," it said.

"I am Stilton, *Geronimo Stilton*," I

The helmet began massaging my scalp.

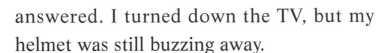

answered. I turned down the TV, but my helmet was still buzzing away.

"It's Professor Paws von Volt," the voice continued. "Geronimo, I need your help!"

I jumped to my paws. Professor von Volt was a brilliant scientist. He was a dear old friend. We had met a long time ago on one of my many adventures. I would do anything for him. Now I strained to hear the professor's words. It sounded like he was in some sort of trouble. "**Where are you, Professor von Volt?**" I cried.

My friend's voice seemed to be growing weaker and weaker. "Geronimo, I'm calling from my secret lab in the Himalayas. I need your help!" he squeaked. "You are the only one I trust! Please go to my house. You'll find the keys under the WELCOME RAT mat. I need you to find my secret diary and bring it to me. It's very important."

I began to twirl my whiskers nervously. The professor's voice was growing fainter by the minute. What had happened? Why did he need my help?

Professor Paws von Volt

"Professor, please speak up," I cried. "I can't hear you."

But it was no use. His voice was fading away. "The diary . . . it's very important . . . found the yeti's pawprints . . . life in danger . . ."

Then the line went dead.

I put down the receiver. I knew I **absolutely** had to help the professor. After all, that's what friends are for!

You Poor Cheesebrain!

Ding...dong...

The doorbell rang again. I went to open it, still wearing my helmet.

It was my sister, Thea. She works as a special correspondent at *The Rodent's Gazette.*

"What on earth are you wearing on your head?" she exclaimed.

I touched my head. I guess I did look A LITTLE SILLY in the helmet. Still, my sister never missed a chance to make fun of me. It was probably her favorite hobby — after going on dates!

"This helmet is going to make my fur grow thicker," I tried to explain.

My sister just snickered.

"The mouse on TV said it really works!" I insisted.

Thea didn't seem convinced. In fact, she began to giggle.

Just then, I remembered the phone call. I grabbed my sister's tail. "Listen, I've got the most **unbelievable news!**" I squeaked. "I just got a call from Professor von Volt. He said something about a **YETI!** You know, the hairy beast that is supposed to live in the Himalayas. Maybe he spotted one!"

Now Thea was really rolling. Rolling with laughter, that is. She was roaring so hard she could barely squeak. "You poor CHEESEBRAIN!" she finally choked out. "How did you get to be such a dimwit? First a helmet that makes your fur grow. Now a **YETI**. It's amazing that we are related!"

I stamped my paw. "But I'm telling you, Thea, it was the professor. He said **HIS LIFE WAS IN DANGER!**" I shrieked.

Thea shook her head. "Really, GERRY BERRY. Everyone knows the yeti is just some silly made-up monster," she sighed. "You need to get out more. You know, get your face out of your encyclopedia once in a while." She **stroked** her fur absentmindedly.

Now I was getting mad. It was one thing to pick on me. But my encyclopedia was priceless!

"Listen, Thea," I insisted. "If Professor von Volt really did find a **YETI**, it would be a great **SCOOP** for the paper. You wouldn't want *The Daily Rat* to get it first, would you?"

My sister rolled her eyes. "I'm telling you, someone is pulling your paw," she said. "Speaking of jokesters, have you seen our cousin Trap lately?"

Sally Ratmousen
the editor of The Daily Rat

Just then, a familiar mouse strolled through my front door. Yes, it was the king of pranks himself, my annoying cousin Trap Stilton.

"What's shakin', *Cousinkins?*" he grinned, jabbing me in the arm. "I heard my name and came scampering." He danced over to my fridge. Then he helped himself to a huge block of cheddar.

There goes breakfast, lunch, and dinner, I fumed to myself.

Thea giggled. "Trap!" she cried. "Did you just play a joke on Geronimo?"

"Cousinkins, I heard my name and came scampering."

THE ABOMINABLE SNOWRAT

My cousin chuckled. "A joke? Which one? I've played so many jokes on Geronimo, I've lost count," he declared. "After all, he's the perfect target. He always falls for it!"

Thea nodded **IMPATIENTLY**. "Well, yes. But I'm talking about a new joke. Someone just called Geronimo and told him he has seen a *YETI*."

Trap snickered under his whiskers. "A *YETI?*" he squeaked. "*Um, interesting* . . . you mean, one of those hairy beasts who live in the mountains?"

I nodded.

"Cousinkins!" Trap shrieked. "I'll let you in on a secret. The **YETI** does not exist! It's **all** made up. Like the Abominable Snowrat. Just a story." For the first time, he seemed to notice the helmet on my head. "What's that thingy covering your peabrain? Are you playing spacemouse? You're a little old for dress-up, don't you think, **GERMEISTER**?"

"Well, I don't care who believes me!" I squeaked. "Professor von Volt needs my help. I'm going off to find him and the **YETI**. **AT LEAST THIS MOUSE KNOWS THE TRUE VALUE OF FRIENDSHIP!**"

For once, my sister and Trap did not let out one squeak. Their jaws HIT THE GROUND.

And do you know why?

Because any mouse who knows me knows *I hate traveling. . . .*

I'm a True Gentlemouse!

Thea twirled her whiskers, peering into my face. "What's the matter, Geronimo?" she said. "Usually I'm the one who wants to travel. I always have to drag you out of your mouse hole kicking and squeaking."

"She's right, Cousin," Trap added. "Um, I think that helmet IS ROASTING YOUR LAST BRAIN CELL. Maybe you should pull the plug."

I went to my closet. I pulled out my luggage. "I know what I'm doing! I am going, and I'm going right now!" I cried. "Professor von Volt needs my help! Unlike you two, I'm a true *gentlemouse*. I don't need you!"

Thea flicked her tail. "So you don't need us, huh?" she smirked.

Trap shook his head. His eyes twinkled. **"He says he doesn't need us,"** he scoffed.

I picked up the phone. I'd show them, I decided. I'd be fine on my own. Nobody could stop me. *"Please send a taxi to Number Eight Mouseford Lane! Right away!"* I squeaked.

I raced into my bedroom. I stuffed a pair of warm pants, a few sweaters, and a **heavy** winter jacket into my suitcase. "It's very cold in the Himalayas," I grumbled, wrapping a wool scarf around my neck.

I closed the suitcase. Then I headed for the door. My cousin and Thea just stared.

"I'm off to the airport. I'll catch the first flight to **KATHMANDU**," I announced *solemnly*.

Then I turned around. "You know, friendship is very important to me," I said. "If a friend asks for my help, I'll do anything for him. I'll even climb Mouse Everest! But if you don't want to come with me, it's all right. I can take care of myself. Good-bye . . . this could be our last farewell!"

What a great exit line. I felt like a real hero. I was brave. I was adventurous. I flung open the door. Yes, I was off on a **DANGEROUS** journey. Off to the cold, treacherous

Himalayan mountain range. **And I was doing it all in the name of friendship.**

What a mouse I am, I told myself. *A mouse of real character.*

Unfortunately, my touching exit was spoiled by my cousin Trap. "Hey, Gerry

Rat!" he called after me. "Maybe you should take off that ridiculous helmet before you leave. You don't want your cab driver laughing too hard. He might drive off the road and crash!"

I turned to make *another speech* but never got the chance. Instead, I tripped over my scarf and **fell flat on my snout**, crushing my whiskers.

I heard Trap chuckling. "Himalayas, my paw!" he laughed. "That stumble mouse will be lucky if he makes it to the airport!!!!"

I'M
LEEEAAAVIIIIINC!!!

I was almost out the door when my favorite nephew, Benjamin, arrived. "Uncle Geronimo!" he squeaked. "Where are you going? Are you leaving?"

"Yes, I am, Benjamin," I answered in a DRAMATIC voice. I wanted to make sure my sister and Trap could hear me. I was hoping they'd change their minds and come along. "Yes, Nephew, I'm off on a journey to a faraway land," I announced. "It's a DANGEROUS place. In fact, I may never come back."

Benjamin's eyes filled with tears. "Please don't go, Uncle," he sobbed. "Or take me with you. I can help you. *I love you so much!*"

I *stroked* his tiny ears. "I'm sorry, Benjamin," I whispered. "I didn't mean to upset you. I'll **come back**, don't worry." Then I cleared my throat. "I must go now. I am off to help a friend. **Wouldn't you do the same?**"

"If you were in trouble, I'd do anything to help!"

Benjamin thought about it for a moment, then nodded. "You're right, Uncle Geronimo," he cried.

My eyes filled with tears. Is he an amazing little mouse or what?

I hugged him tightly and headed for the taxi.

I noticed Thea and Trap watching me.

"*I am leaving!*" I announced SOLEMNLY. They just watched.

I opened the taxi's door. *"I'm leaving!"* WELL, WHAT WERE THEY WAITING FOR? I thought for sure they would insist on coming with me. We practically always went on adventures together. It wouldn't be the same without them. Thea is so **courageous**, and Trap always knows how to get us out of a jam.

Maybe I'd gone a little overboard with the "I'll do it myself" bit. I kept the door open just in case. But they only stared at me.

"Well, I'm off! I mean it. **I'M really leaving!**" I called.

Not a word. The silence was killing me. I'd never felt so alone in my whole life. Well, there was that one time when I got lost on my way back from Cheese Mart. I ended up at Purrfect Park. There wasn't a mouse in sight. Just cats. Lots of **CATS**. But that's another story. . . .

Right now, I just wanted someone to say something. Anything. I'd even take a "We'll miss you!" Still, I did not hear one squeak.

"I'm leaving and I may never come back!" I **SHRIEKED**. "I could end up in the jaws of a mountain lion! Or my tail

"*I'm leaaaviiiiiiiing!*"

could freeze right off! Yep, I'm headed for dangerous territory! Here I go!"

NO REACTION.

I climbed into the taxi and shut the door. Then I rolled down the window.

"*I'm leaaaaviiiiiiiiiiiiing!*"

I squeaked **AT THE TOP OF MY LUNGS**. "This mouse is history!" I tried to look brave and strong. But inside I felt like a

I'm leaaaviiiiiiiing!

bowl of my great-grandma Tanglefur's gooey cream cheese. I couldn't believe it. Would they **really** let me go off on my own? How would I manage? What if I snapped a whisker? Or even worse, what if I lost my glasses? I wouldn't be able to see a thing. I pictured myself asking a mountain lion for directions. Then I'd really be history. I started to shake with fear. Who was I kidding? I couldn't go on this trip alone.

With a sob, I jumped out of the taxi. "Holey cheese! I don't want to leave on my own!" I cried. "I need my family!"

Thea ran **TOWARD ME** and wrapped me in a furry hug. "Don't worry, big brother," she said. "I'll meet you at the airport in ten minutes!"

Trap gave me a friendly slap on the shoulder. Well, OK, it was more like a hard

I'M  LEEEAAAVIIIIIING!!!

Nothing beats being with your family.

punch, but this time I didn't mind. "**Cousinkins**," he said. "I still don't believe the story about the **YETI**, but I'll come along. After all, you'd never make it without me. You'd probably turn into ᴄᴀᴛ ꜰᴏᴏᴅ in no time flat!"

Benjamin grabbed my paw. "I'm coming too, Uncle!" he beamed. "I'll help you fight those rotten cats!"

I grinned. Nothing beats being with your family.

The taxi rat driver just shrugged and shook his head. "**Crazy** mice," he muttered. "You never know if they're coming or going."

Taxirat driver

I HATE TRAVELING!

I took the taxi straight to Professor von Volt's house. After I got my paws on his diary, I met everyone at the airport. Soon we were headed for Kathmandu in the heart of NEPAL. From there, we climbed aboard a tiny, rickety plane. It dropped us off in the middle of a small green valley.

By then, my stomach was doing somersaults. You see, I have a little problem with airplanes. They make me terribly sick.

Of course, because I felt ill, Trap decided to pick on me. He began singing in a silly voice:

"We've just landed in Kathmandu,
And Gerrytail's stomach is in a stew!
Yes, airplanes can turn him green,
It's the funniest sight you've ever seen.
Fast cars and bikes can make him groan,
It's a wonder he goes anywhere on his own!
He's such a wimp as you can see,
I can hardly believe he's related to me!"

I was **FUMING**. It was just like my cousin to kick a mouse when he's down.

Just then, a rodent with **honey-colored** fur and a black ponytail approached us. "Are you the Stiltons? I'm **RATFUR**, your Sherpa guide!" he declared.

He and his four helpers picked up our luggage. *Our adventure was about to begin!*

My heart began to race. But this time it wasn't from nerves. I was excited. I could hardly wait to start exploring. I looked around.

FAR AWAY, THE SNOWCAPPED MOUNTAINS SEEMED TO GLOW A MAGICAL WHITE. . . .

BOILING HOT TEA AND YAK CHEESE

We reached a small inn. Our new friends unloaded the luggage, and **WE WENT IN**.

It looked sort of like a ski lodge inside. Rodents wearing warm hats and heavy coats sat around **WOODEN TABLES**, munching cheese. Others were squeaking away by the fire. The whole place was lit by oil lamps that cast an eerie glow on the room.

I cleared my throat. "We are looking for a middle-aged rodent with orangish-brown fur," I told our guide. "He's not very tall and he wears glasses."

We reached a small inn.

Ratfur nibbled **SOME CHEESE** and took a few sips of **boiling** hot tea. "**Ummm,** not very tall, you say? With orangish-brown fur? Wearing glasses?" he mumbled. "Say, I think I saw a rodent like him about six months ago."

The inn

I was very excited. "**You saw him? Where did he go? Please tell me,** it's a matter of life or death!" I squeaked.

Ratfur nibbled away on **another piece of cheese**. "Isn't this the best stuff?" he remarked. "It's yak cheese. *Have you ever seen a yak?* They look like bulls, but their horns are long and curved. They are **tame** and useful beasts. They

A yak

give us **MILK**, fur, and fat. See the lamp over there? It uses **Yak** fat."

I waited impatiently. I didn't want to rush our guide. If I got under his fur, he might not want to tell me anything.

After nine more nibbles of cheese and fifteen more sips of tea, Ratfur sat back. Then he grabbed my paw and began to whisper.

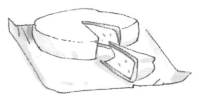

Yak cheese

"Okay, here's the **SCOOP**," he began. "The mouse you mentioned didn't want anyone to know where he was going. But I heard him say something about **CHOMOLUNGMA**."

"Chomolungma?" I asked with a sigh of relief. "Well, in that case, finding him should be as easy as **RUNNING** up a clock! All we have to do is go to Chomolungma! By the way, how far is Chomolungma from here?"

Ratfur gave me a funny look.

"You can't go to Chomolungma," he squeaked.

Yak-fat-burning Lamp

"**Why?**" I asked, surprised.

"You've got to **CLIMB** Chomolungma! It's the Mother of the World!"

I scratched my head. "The Mother of the World?" I asked.

Ratfur nodded. "Tibetans call it Chomolungma, the MOTHER OF THE WORLD," he explained. "But you call it **MOUSE EVEREST!!!**"

THE STORY OF A LIFETIME!

We all gasped. Mouse Everest is the highest mountain in the world! I felt **faint**.

"Mouse Everest?" Thea squeaked. "This sounds like the story of a lifetime! Let's go!"

Benjamin threw his paws around my neck. "Holey cheese, Uncle!" he shrieked. "We're going to climb Mouse Everest!"

Trap began stuffing his snout with food. "Hey, this yak cheese is pretty tasty," he remarked. "But I'll need something more filling if I'm going to scurry up that big old hill."

I was still in SHOCK! SHOCK! SHOCK!

29,028 feet

"Big old hill?" I cried. "Mouse Everest is 29,028 feet high! I'll never make it."

Ratfur didn't seem to hear me. "We can leave right now, if you want," he said.

"R-r-r-ight n-n-ow?" I stammered. "Maybe we should think about it first." Um...

Um... Um... Um...

But I was talking to myself. The others were already outside.

Ratfur headed toward a narrow, steep path. It went up and up and up. I got dizzy just looking at it! My paws felt like JELLY. In case you haven't guessed, I'm really not much of a sportsmouse.

Ratfur turned and waved for us to follow. The others quickly marched ahead in the **suffocating** heat and humidity. They were squeaking with excitement.

Oh, what had I gotten myself into **this time?**

I'm a Squeaky Weakling

The path *climbed higher and higher.*

My mood *sank lower and lower.*

We climbed for an hour, then two, then three.

After a while, the sun began to sink. Still, Ratfur kept going! Was he trying to get into the *Guinness Book of Mouse Records*?

I was about to collapse! My whiskers were dripping with SWEAT. My backpack weighed a **TON**. I felt like I was carting twenty bricks of my aunt Swissella's rock-hard fruitcake. One Christmouse, I used one of her cakes as a paperweight! But I kept climbing. I couldn't let Professor von Volt down. He was counting on me. I had to keep going, even if I pulled every muscle in my body.

I glanced up ahead. My sister was practically sk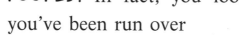ipping along. She's the real sportsmouse in the family. She didn't even look like she was out of breath! What a show-off.

Just then, Trap sneaked up beside me. "Cousin," he squeaked in my ear. "You're looking a little pooped. No, make that a lot POOPED. In fact, you look like you've been run over

by a cheese truck on the freeway!" He started laughing loudly. *Hee-hee!*

His laughter echoed down the mountain. Then he leaned in close. "Don't sweat it, Gerrytails," he grinned. "You can't help it if you've got a jelly belly. Here's a little trick to keep you going. Just repeat after me: *"I, Geronimo Stilton, can make it, I can make it . . ."*

I was so tired, I was ready to take advice from anyone. Yes, even from my obnoxious cousin Trap. I repeated his words, "**I, Geronimo Stilton, can make it, I can make it . . .**"

Trap went on, still smirking, "*. . . even if I'm a squeaky weakling, even if I'm a squeaky weakling . . .*"

I repeated, "*. . . even if I'm a squeaky weakling . . .*"

Suddenly, I realized he was making fun of me. "How dare you call me a SQUEAKY WEAKLING!" I squeaked. I would have pinched his tail, but my paws felt too weak.

Trap just laughed harder. Then he SPRINTED away to join the others.

I could hear him singing:

"*Shake your paw, swing your tail,*

You're lagging behind like a tired snail!
Here comes the train, ding-ding-ding,
Come on, move it, squeaky weakling!"

I sighed. Thank goodness for my sweet nephew Benjamin. He had decided to walk beside me to cheer me up.

"Don't mind him, Uncle Geronimo," Benjamin said. "You are not a squeaky weakling!"

I forced a tired smile. "Thank you, Benjamin. You're the only one who understands me," I panted.

understands me. Thank you, Benjamin. You're the only one who

I'm Too Fond of
My Tail!

Before long, it was dark. We got ready to spend our first night on the mountain.

It was unbelievably **COLD**.

I wrapped up warmly from whiskers to tail. I took special care with my tail. I didn't want it to freeze. **I'm too fond of my tail!**

RATFUR

We made a dinner of boiled rice and yak cheese.

Trap made a face. "Yak! Yak! Yak!"

he grumbled. "There's nothing but yak cheese around here. This mouse cannot live on yak alone! I need a little variety in my diet." He began to sing *dreamily*:

"Mozzarella, parmesan,
Don't forget the cheddar.
Goat cheese, Swiss cheese,
Any of these are better!
There are so many cheeses,
Why stick to just one?
When tasting all different kinds
Is really half the fun!"

Then he winked at me. "At least we've got a little jelly," he grinned. "Yep, our very own jelly belly!" THEN HE POINTED AT ME. EVERYONE LAUGHED. All except Benjamin.

I'm Feeling Faint with Fear!

The next morning, Ratfur woke us up at the crack of dawn. What was for breakfast? You guessed it, **Yak** cheese and **boiling** hot tea!

I had spent an **AWFUL** night. I had tossed and turned in my too-tight sleeping bag. I felt like a giant caterpillar stuck in an extra-small cocoon. I was **ACHING ALL OVER!**

I stuck my snout outside my tent and **SHIVERED**. *Frozen frogs' legs!* It was colder

I had tossed and turned all night...

than the inside of an ice-cheese truck. Even my eyeballs were freezing! Luckily, I could still see out of them. When I glanced up, I saw an amazing sight. Over the horizon, the sun lit up the snow-covered peaks. Everything sparkled. I was spellbound.

Ratfur pointed to one of the peaks. "Over there is Chomolungma, the Mother of the World," he told us.

Benjamin grabbed my paw. "Isn't it unbelievable, Uncle?" he squeaked.

I *stroked* his tiny ears. "Yes, my dear nephew," I murmured. "It really is a sight for frozen eyes."

I wish we could have relaxed and enjoyed the view. But Ratfur shouted, "Let's go!"

We marched all day long. *In between the mountain peaks*, we had to cross through the rain forest. I heard the **ROAR** of a waterfall in the distance.

The lush forest was SUPER HUMID. We pushed through a tangle of ferns and thick bamboo trees. Then we passed the ROARING WATERFALL.

After a while, I found myself in front of a wooden bridge. But this wasn't just any wooden bridge. It was a L-O-N-G wooden bridge. It was longer than the Twisted Tail

Gate Bridge. That's the longest bridge on Mouse Island!

Are you afraid of heights? I am!

Brrrrrrr!!! Brrrrrrr!!! Brrrrrrr!!!

I turned as PALE as a slice of mozzarella. "Couldn't we go across somewhere else?" I mumbled.

Thea **HURRIED** past me, snickering. "Come on, you 'fraidy mouse," she squeaked. "There's nothing to it!"

She took Benjamin by the paw, and they started along the bridge. He turned around to look back at me. "I'll be waiting for you at the other end, Uncle Geronimo," he whispered.

They reached the other side in no time. Benjamin waved to me. "Come on, Uncle!" he called. "It's real easy!"

My whiskers were quivering with fear. I stared at the long, empty bridge swinging in the wind.

I stepped onto the bridge. Slowly, I placed one paw in front of the other.

Suddenly, I felt the bridge swaying. I turned around. It was Trap. "Last one

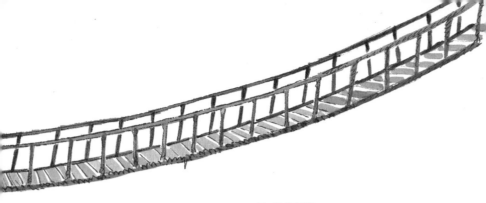

across is **A ROTTEN RAT!**" he shrieked, slapping me on the back.

With a terrified squeak, I grabbed the rope railing. Far, far below I saw a tiny stream in the middle of a canyon. Jagged rocks jutted out on either side. I felt faint with fear. One wrong pawstep and my fur would be plastered all over those rocks!

"**CRUNCHY CHEESE BITS!** Don't mOvE!" I begged my cousin.

Of course, I should have known that would set him off. He began jumping up and down like a mad mouse. Then he turned a few *somersaults*.

As he jumped, my cousin began to sing:

La la la ... La la la ... La la la ... La la la ...

"Don't look down, it's much too scary!
Watch that step, be very wary!
Poor Geronimo, you're such a cheesehead,
You get dizzy when you climb out of bed!"

He **ZOOMED** past me. My stomach churned with fear. I hoped I wasn't going to blow cheese chunks on the bridge.

Very carefully, I began to inch forward. At last, I reached the other side. I was so proud of myself. **I DID IT!**

But my victory didn't last long. Farther up the path I heard my sister shouting. "GeronimOOO! Are you taking a ratnap?" she screeched. "Let's go, we're all waiting!"

I sighed.

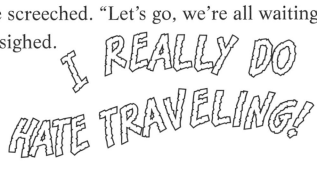
I REALLY DO HATE TRAVELING!

A GIGANTIC PAWPRINT!

A week went by.

I was getting so tired, I could hardly blink. The weather didn't help. It was COLDER than a deep-freeze cheddar slushy at The Icy Rat.

Yes, we had left the lush green valleys behind. Now we stumbled over rocky canyons covered in LAYERS of ICE.

Finally, we reached the path that led to the bottom of Mouse Everest.

The snow whirled around us in mini-windstorms.

Brrrrrrr!!! Brrrrrrr!!. Brrrrrrr!!!

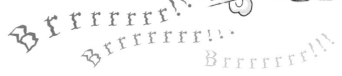

I did my best to stay with the group. But they were all so much faster than me. Before long, *I FOUND MYSELF ALONE.*

And that's when I saw it.

A GIGANTIC pawprint in the snow.

I cleaned my glasses. Could it be? Could it really be? I bent closer to get a better look.

Crumbling cheddar cheese crisps!

My fur stood on end. It was the **YETI**'s pawprint! I just knew it!

"Found the yeti's pawprints . . . life in danger . . ." Professor von Volt had said.

I could hardly believe it. I was so excited I forgot about the cold. I even forgot about being tired. I'd found the **YETI**! My friend had to be nearby!

"The yeti!" I squeaked, jumping up and down. "Come quick!"

But the others couldn't hear me. They were already too F A R   A W A Y.

Too Much Yak Cheese

I took a huge breath. Then I shrieked at the top of my lungs, *"Thea! Trap! I've found the yeti!!!"*

Luckily, this time, they heard me. They turned and stared at me. Their mouths **dropped open**.

Then they burst out LAUGHING. *Ha! Ha! Ha!*

I was hurt. "You don't believe me?" I squeaked. "I'm telling you, I found a pawprint! Come see for yourselves!"

Trap just chuckled. "Cousin, are you seeing double? Maybe you should lay off the yak cheese for a while."

I WAS GETTING ANNOYED.

Thea rolled her eyes. "OK," she agreed. "I'll come take a look. If it's really there, it would be a *fabumouse* scoop." She grabbed her digital camera. "But you'd better not be pulling my paw," she added.

We turned back.

Meanwhile, the **SNOW** kept falling. Of course, I should have known. By the time we reached the spot where I'd seen the pawprint . . .

. . IT WASN'T THERE ANYMORE!

The **SNOW** must have covered it up!

Meanwhile, the snow kept falling.

Meanwhile, the snow kept falling.

Meanwhile, the snow kept falling.

Meanwhile, the snow kept falling.

Meanwhile, the snow kept falling.

Did You See an Unidentified Flying Cheese Slice?

Trap began sniggering under his whiskers. "Cousinkins, were you wearing your glasses when you saw this pawprint?" he giggled. "How long was it? Two feet, ten feet, twenty, a **mile**? Did you see any other interesting thingamajigs out there? Like, for example . . .

AN UNIDENTIFIED FLYING CHEESE SLICE?"

I stamped my paw. But just as I opened my mouth to squeak, my sister piped up.

"Geronimo," Thea snarled. "It's too cold for this kind of joke! The next time you see a pawprint, keep it to yourself!"

I saw Ratfur watching us. He turned to the other Sherpa guides and began speaking *RAPIDLY*. "Yeti . . . yeti . . ." I heard them whispering. I wondered if they believed me.

I saw a yeti's pawprint, I really did!

A Mysterious Shadow in the Fog

We continued **TRUDGING UP** the mountain. The **ICY** wind sliced through my fur. I was exhausted! I was having trouble just breathing! You see, the higher you climb, the less oxygen there is in the air.

I plodded along, dragging my paws. My **heavy** backpack was crushing me. I felt like I had been running the New Mouse City Marathon for weeks with ten rats strapped to my back.

The only thing that kept me going was the professor. I knew we were getting closer to his hidden laboratory. *The dear old professor.* He never stayed in one place for too long. That way, no one could steal his secret discoveries. I was the only one to know each new address. The professor trusted me. I would never give away personal information. Yep, I can hold my tongue when I need to. In fact, I would probably make a good spy mouse.

Lost in my thoughts, I didn't realize I had dropped behind.

From off in the distance, I heard Trap singing:

"Geronimo has vanished in the mist,
How do we know if he still exists?
Maybe he was so very smelly.
He's now inside the yeti's belly!"

I PICKED UP MY PACE. It was hard to find my way through the snowy fog.

And then I saw it. A **tall**, dark, **HUMONGOUS** shadow appeared before my eyes!

The shadow seemed to be waving to me.

I felt faint. It was the **YETI!!!**

My whiskers were quivering with fear.

Seconds later, the mysterious shadow disappeared.

A tall, dark, humongous shadow appeared before my eyes!

PEEKABOO! I'M A YETI, WHAT ARE YOU?

I ran to catch up with the group.

"The ye-yeti! I saw the yeti!" I stammered. **"I SAW ITS SHADOW IN THE FOG.** Then it disappeared."

Thea shook her head. **"How come you're the only one to see it?"** she grumbled. She took her camera and slapped it into my paw.

"Here you are! Next time take a picture!"  she yelled. **"I ABSOLUTELY NEED SOME HOT STUFF FOR THE PAPER.** I need a scoop. I can't go back empty-pawed!"

Trap was singing again:

"This yeti seems a bit cuckoo,
He's into playing peekaboo.
Only Geronimo can see him,
But no one will believe him,
Because he lies with such ease,
He's even seen a flying cheese!"

I pretended not to hear him. The more ANGRY I got, the more Trap enjoyed it.

Trap jumped from one rock to the next, MAKING FACES at me.

"Peekaboo... peekaboo...I'm a yeti, what are you?" Once again, I pretended not to hear. Disappointed, Trap gave up.

Benjamin winked at me. "Good idea, Uncle Geronimo," he whispered. "Maybe if you ignore him, he'll stop *pulling your paw*."

Just then, Ratfur appeared at my side. **"Ummm, what did the shadow look like? How tall was it?"** he asked.

I described it as best I could.

He seemed to be lost in thought. Soon he was jabbering away with his Sherpa friends. "Yeti . . . **YETI** . . . !" I heard them murmuring. YETI! YETI! YETI! YETI!

We stopped to camp for the night. The sun had already set. What mysteries lurked in the darkness?

I tried to work things out logically. Why did the **YETI** appear only to me? Was there a reason? I had a sudden thought. I had to find the yeti. If I found it, I would also find Professor von Volt.

Just then, I heard a shout.

"Uhhh-uuuuuuuuuuuuuh!!!"

Ratfur and his friends turned PALE.
"Yeti . . . yeti . . ." they murmured.

Thea sprinted off in search of the mysterious shouter.

I grabbed the camera Thea had given me. "Wait for me here," I told Benjamin. "Don't leave the camp, no matter what!"

I took a deep breath. I was scared out of my wits. But I had to go. I had to find my friend. With a shiver, I scampered into the darkness.

"Professor von Volt, I'M ON MY WAY!"
I called.

ICICLES ON MY WHISKERS

Once again, I heard the shout.

"Uhhhh-uuuuuuuuh!!!"

I followed the sound as I ju m ped from rock to rock. Who says I'm no sportsmouse?
Let's see Trap make fun of me now, I said to myself, grinning. Then I immediately sli pp ed and f ell headfirst into a PILE OF SNOW.

When I got up, my whiskers were covered in ICICLES. I realized I was far away from our camp.

Suddenly, I saw it. It was a pawprint half covered in snow. A bit farther away I saw another one, and then one more!

"Benjamin! Thea! Trap!" I cried.

No one answered. I gulped. What if I couldn't find my way back to camp? I couldn't spend a night on this icy cold mountain all alone. I'd end up one frozen mousicle!

I decided to follow the tracks. Maybe if I kept going I could find Professor von Volt.

I made my way in the darkness, pawstep by pawstep. Then the tracks *suddenly* stopped. I was about to turn back when I heard a strange creaking.

Benjamin... ...amiin! ...amiin!

Thea... ...eaaaaaaa! ...eaaaaaaa!

Trap... ...aaaaaaap! ...aaaaaaap! ...aaaaaaap!

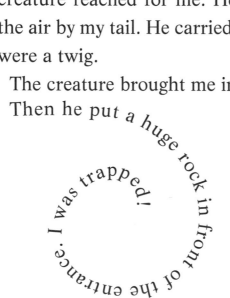

The rock in front of me was beginning to move. I looked up and saw a **HUMONGOUS** creature lifting it to one side.

If only I could move my paws. But I was frozen. This time, it wasn't the cold that had me shivering. I was FROZEN WITH FEAR!

Before I could think of what to do, the big creature reached for me. He lifted me into the air by my tail. He carried me away as if I were a twig.

The creature brought me into a dark cave. Then he put a huge rock in front of the entrance. I was trapped!

He lifted me into the air by my tail.

TAKE THAT,
YOU BIG BRUTE!

I clutched at the yeti's **furry** paw. I had to do something . . . and *FAST*! The big guy looked hungry. I didn't want to become his bedtime snack! Quickly, and with all of my might, I chomped down on one of his fingers. *"Take that, you big brute!"* I squeaked.

The yeti howled in pain. Then he *dropped* me to the floor.

I scampered away, quiet as a mouse. **The cave was so dark.** I hid behind a rock.

The creature looked around for a while. Finally, he gave up and left. He lumbered deeper into the cave. His **heavy** steps made the walls shake.

I followed him. Oh, yes, I was terrified. But I am still a newspaper mouse at heart. I had to see what the strange creature was up to. I had to get the story.

In the meantime, I studied the cave. It was dark, gloomy, . . and VERY HUMID. Drops of water fell on my ears from above.

PLINK PLINK PLINK . . . PLINK PLINK PLINK

I kept a safe distance between myself and the yeti. I may be a newspaper mouse, but I'm not crazy. I needed to live to tell this tale.

Just then, the cave **became wider**. I almost let out an *Oooooh!* of surprise. The walls were

PLINK PLINK PLINK PLINK

PLINK

covered in sheets of ICE. Thousands of sparkling STALACTITES hung from the ceiling.

It looked like a ballroom in a beautiful fairy-tale castle. I could just see Cinderatella dancing by with Prince Charming. In one corner, there was a small GURGLING WATERFALL. It s p r e a d into a pool of crystal-clear water.

I realized this was the yeti's den. He was waving excitedly at something or someone. *"Yooooo-hoooo!!"* he called out happily.

At the other end of the cave, I saw another shadow wave its paw. *"Yooooo-hoooo!!"* Weird!

Who would have guessed? The yeti had a WIFE!

PROFESSOR
VON VOLT

I moved forward to get a better look. The **YETI** was very tall and had **THICK CLAWS**. He was covered from head to paw in long, snowy white **FUR**. *No danger of going bald here,* I thought. The yeti looked like a **WALKING SHAG CARPET!**

His wife was the spitting image of him, just smaller and **rounder**. I watched as she ran and PuLLeD HiM TOWARD the other end of the cave. There I spotted a snug little nest in the snow. In the middle of the nest was a mound of white fur.

Just then, the fur began to sob loudly. My mouth hung open. I felt like my cousin Cheddar at his surprise birthday party. It was a **yeti cub!**

"**Gniiik- gniiiiik!!!**" shrieked the cub. His mother placed a tender kiss on his snout. It worked like a charm. He immediately grew quiet.

It was then that I noticed something odd about the cub. He was covered in small **red dots**. Could yetis get the chicken pox? I stared in amazement.

Suddenly, a familiar figure appeared out of nowhere. I forgot all about being quiet. "**Professor von Volt!**" I shouted.

He quickly spun around. "*Geronimo Stilton!*" he exclaimed, grinning.

LULLABY FOR A SICK YETI

I *RAN* to the professor's rescue.

"Don't worry, Professor! I'm here to save you!" I squeaked. Yes, I, *Geronimo Stilton*, would fight those big, hairy yetis until the finish! And I would do it all for my dear friend Professor von Volt!

The professor just stared at me. He seemed confused. At last, he smiled.

"It's OK, Geronimo," he squeaked. "I'm not the one in danger."

I blinked. Now I was the one to look confused. What was going on? Hadn't the professor sent for me because he was in danger? Isn't that why I had just traveled all the way to ICY COLD Mouse Everest?

Just then, I saw the professor was holding A GLASS BOTTLE of green LIQUID in his paw.

He poured some of the liquid into a spoon made of bone. Then he fed it to the young yeti. "Drink your medicine, little one," he murmured. "Soon you'll be as strong as your dad and as beautiful as your mom."

The cub made a face. "Bleaaahhh!!!" he cried, shaking his head. But eventually he gulped down the liquid. Then he closed his eyes and curled up snugly in the snow.

His mother stroked his fur as she sang a tune. It sounded like a lullaby. Soon, the cub was snoring away.

Professor von Volt pulled me aside. "I believe I owe you an explanation, Geronimo," he whispered. "You see, I am not the one in DANGER," he began. "This baby yeti is. He is very ill. I sent his father in search of you. That's why you're the only one who saw him. I hope he didn't fluster you too much. He's huge, but he's quite *mild-mannered*."

I stared at the enormous hairy creature. No, the father yeti hadn't flustered me. He had scared me half to death! He had knocked ten years off my natural mouse lifespan! But I didn't want to make the professor feel bad. "Oh, no, I thought the **YETI** seemed quite friendly," I lied.

Professor von Volt smiled and continued his tale. "As I was building my secret lab in this cave, I discovered a family of yetis," he explained. "You see, dear Geronimo, many thousands of years ago, the Himalayan mountains were populated by tribes of yetis. The yetis are **HERBIVORES**, which means they do not eat meat. They wouldn't hurt a fly! Then, gradually, almost all of the yetis were wiped out by a

illness."

A True Gentlemouse!

"These three you see here are the last surviving yetis in the **Himalayas!**" Professor von Volt went on. He stared fondly at the cub. "I've been trying to cure this little guy with an herbal medicine. **BUT IT'S NOT STRONG ENOUGH**," he said, shaking his head. "That's why I needed my secret diary. It contains a **SPECIAL FORMULA** that just might work."

I sprang to my paws and dug through my backpack. I found the diary and pawed it over to the professor. "Here you go!" I squeaked.

He took it, heaving a sigh of relief. "Oh, **thank you**, Geronimo," he squeaked. "You have no idea how much this means to me!"

Minutes later, he had found the page with the **SECRET FORMULA**. He grabbed a test tube and set to work. I smiled. Professor von Volt loves working in his laboratory as much as I love reading a first-rat book!

After a while, the professor held up a bottle. *"This will do the trick!"* he announced.

He fed the young **YETI** a spoonful of the new medicine. Then he took my paw in his. "My dear Geronimo," he said. "Thanks to you, we have just saved the last existing **YETI** cub!"

I felt a twinge of pride. Maybe I wasn't the bravest or the strongest mouse on the block.

And maybe I wasn't even the best **sportsmouse**. OK, I admit it. I am always the last rodent picked for the team. But I was something even better. I was a good friend!

"There's something I need to tell you, Geronimo," the professor said. "Six months ago, I had set up my lab on a small desert island in the RATLANTIC OCEAN. But then someone tried to steal my latest invention, a time-travel machine. So I was forced to move to this cave. But someone is still after my secrets. I've decided to move the lab again to a submarine. We'll see if . . ."

Ratlantic Ocean

"A submarine!" I squeaked. The professor sure was one well-traveled mouse!

"My dear friend, I am very glad I got to see you again. But I need just one more favor," the professor continued, lowering his voice. "I know the discovery of yetis would be a sensational scoop. But I would be grateful if you did not tell anyone about their existence. They are extremely **SHY** creatures. They would be deeply upset by

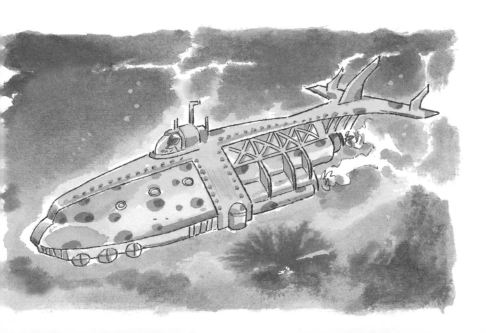

nosy journalists. What do you say, Geronimo?"

I placed a paw on my heart. "Of course, Professor," I agreed. "I give you my rodent's word of honor. You can count on me!"

He chuckled. Then he wrapped me in a furry hug. "You are a true *gentlemouse!*" he squeaked.

Rodent's word of honor

GNIIIK-GNIIIK!!!!

Professor von Volt packed his things. Then he shook hands with the father yeti, who moved the **ROCK** that hid the entrance.

Outside of the cave, I saw a helicopter the color of Swiss cheese. The professor climbed into the pilot's seat and switched on the engines.

The helicopter began to rise in the air. A **HUGE** steel box dangled from the bottom. It contained all of the professor's lab equipment.

Professor von Volt waved his paw. "Good-bye, Geronimo! I hope to see you soon, dear friend!" he called out.

Good-bye!

Soon, the helicopter was just a speck in the sky.

The yetis peeked out of the cave. I think they were sad to see the professor leave. I

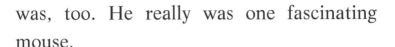

was, too. He really was one fascinating mouse.

Before I headed out, I took one last look at the yetis. It was too bad I wouldn't be able to tell anyone about them. But I had promised the professor. And a rodent's promise is a promise.

Just then, I noticed the little cub peeking out from his mother's paws. "Get well soon, little guy," I whispered.

Then the most amazing thing happened. The cub lifted his little paw and waved at me! "Gniiik-gniiik!!!!" he chirped.

"Holey cheese!" I laughed, waving back at him. Maybe telling the world about the yetis wasn't the most important thing after all.

An Unbelievable Sight

I wasn't looking forward to my trip back. How would I ever find my way to camp? I could barely see my own whiskers in front of my face!

"Heeelp! Heeeelp!"

I shrieked in a panic.

I wandered around, for who knows how long. Minutes? Hours? Oh, how I longed to be back home!

Just when I was beginning to lose all hope, I spotted a dim light. I ran toward it, squeaking with glee.

Suddenly, Benjamin's snout appeared out

of the fog. "Uncle! Uncle Geronimo! You're safe!" he squeaked. *"I was so worried about you."*

I hugged him tight. "Oh, how I missed you, dear nephew," I cried. "I love you *so much*. But why are you out here? It's dangerous."

Benjamin hung his head. He knew I had told him not to leave camp. "We were worried you wouldn't find your way back," he explained, twisting his tail. "When nobody was looking, I took a lamp and went searching for you. I know it was wrong," he admitted.

I put my paw around my nephew and told him everything was OK. Then, chattering happily, we headed for camp.

A few minutes later, we passed **BY A STEEP ICY CLIFF**. Out of the corner of my eye, I noticed a **dark** shape outlined in the ice.

I stopped for a closer look. Big snowflakes **WHIRLED** around me, blurring my sight.

The **STEEP CLIFF** was terrifying. Still, I was determined to find out more. Yes, the newspaper mouse in me was taking over. I had to get the scoop!

I urged Benjamin to stay put. Then, quivering with fear, I climbed up onto an enormous rock. Very carefully, I leaned toward the block of **ICE**. I brushed off the snow. The shape began to emerge. With shaking paws, I brushed off more snow. I could hardly believe my eyes! I, *Geronimo Stilton*, was peering right

into the face of a woolly mammoth! He was perfectly preserved within the ICE!

What a find! I tried to remember what I knew about the woolly mammoth. *It was a prehistoric animal that looked like an elephant, only smaller. It had two very long tusks and thick brown fur. It became extinct toward the end of the Pleistocene Age, around 11,000 years ago.*

I grabbed Thea's camera out of my backpack and snapped some shots. *snap! snap! snap!* This time, no one would think I was making up crazy mouse stories!

Back at camp, Thea rushed out to meet me. "So did you find him?" she demanded. "Did you get a picture of the yeti?"

I shook my head.

Thea groaned. "It figures," she grumbled.
Trap swaggered over. "Well, what a surprise, **GERRY BERRY**," he scoffed. "All the time I thought you saw the yeti. Sometimes here, sometimes there, sometimes in your underwear!"

I just shook my head, smiling. *We'll see who has the last laugh, Mr. Jokester.*

"No, I did not find the yeti," I said, sighing; then I paused for dramatic effect. **"But I did find a woolly mammoth!"**

I took out the digital camera and showed them the pictures of the frozen beast.

For once, Trap did not make one wisecrack. In fact, he seemed to have lost his voice. He opened his mouth, but not a single squeak came out.

Finally, he pulled himself together. "A woolly

mammoth?" he gasped. "Geronimo found a

MAMM⊙TH???"

Thea was jumping for joy. "Now, this is what I call a real **scoop!** I can't wait to write this up. *The Rodent's Gazette* will sell like hotcakes!" she shrieked. "Just think how furious Sally Ratmousen, the editor of *The Daily Rat,* is going to be."

"Uncle Geronimo is the bravest mouse ever," Benjamin squeaked. "You should have seen him climb up that icy cliff!"

That night, we happily nibbled away at our dinners. No one even complained about the yak cheese. We were all too excited about my big discovery.

Later, as I was about to fall asleep, Benjamin grabbed my paw. "Tell me the

truth, `Uncle Geronimo`," he whispered.
"`Did you see the yeti?`"

I could not lie to the little mouse. "Dear Benjamin, I did see him," I whispered back. "But he has a right to be left in peace. I think we should not tell anyone about him. It will be our little secret, OK?"

Benjamin smiled. He put his small paw on his heart. "Of course, Uncle," he said softly. "We won't tell anyone! On my rodent's word of honor!"

Rodent's word of honor!

PICTURE THIS . . .

We started on our way back. Lucky for me, it was all downhill. My paws couldn't take any more climbing.

As soon as we reached **KATHMANDU**, Thea sent out a special report. It would be front-page news.

At last, our plane landed on Mouse Island. A crowd of photographers was already waiting for us.

"Mr. Stilton, a question, please!"

"How did you find the mammoth?"

"Geronimo! Would you care to give an interview to *JOPJW*?" they called out.

Trap tried to answer in my place. He loved

being in the spotlight. "Why don't you interview me?" he suggested. "I was there, too, you know."

But the journalists didn't give him a second glance.

"Please, listen, everyone!" I said. "I would like to dedicate this discovery to Professor Paws von Volt. Unfortunately, he cannot be with us today."

Then I began to tell my story. "When I found the WOOLLY MAMMOTH in the block of ice, I was with my nephew Benjamin. . . ."

Benjamin was drowned in photographs.

I put my paw around Thea. "My sister has filmed a wonderful piece, which will be shown on television this evening. . . ."

click! *click!* *click!* Everyone took pictures of Thea. Just then, my secretary, Mousella, made her way through the crowd. "Mr. Stilton!" she yelled. "Today's edition has sold out! It's an absolute **RECORD!**"

Through the crowd, I saw the face of Sally Ratmousen, editor of *The Daily Rat*. She was green with envy at my success!

"*Mr. Stilton!*" squeaked a gray rat with a camera. "*Could we take your picture?*"

Out of the corner of my eye, I caught a glimpse of my cousin. He was standing all by himself. He looked sad and lonely.

A wave of kindness rushed over me. I know he can be a rotten pain in my fur, but

Trap is still my relative. And my friend.

I turned to the rat with the camera. "I would be happy to have my picture taken. But I would like all of my family members to be with me." Then I waved Trap over.

My cousin was thrilled. He threw his paws around me. And that's when the photographer snapped the picture.

Trap began to sing happily:

"What a sensational success,
We're the darlings of the press!
Despite the cold and the stress,
My cousin made it nonetheless!"

BACK TO THE FUTURE!

Several months went by. The WOOLLY MAMMOTH was brought back to Mouse Island.

Would you believe it? The entire BLOCK OF ICE was cut from the mountain. It was hauled back to the island aboard a special freezer ship!

The MAMMOTH was donated to New Mouse City's Mouseum of Natural History. There it was defrosted and studied by several scientists. It was found to be a valuable source of information about life in the PLEISTOCENE AGE.

Finally, it was exhibited to the public for everyone to admire. **The line for the mouseum stretched for three blocks!** It was like the time the blockbuster *Supermouse IV* opened at the Grand Squeak Cinema.

The exhibition's success gave me an idea. I wrote a book about dinosaurs, mammoths, and other prehistoric animals. It became A BESTSELLER!

More months went by.

One morning, as I was checking my e-mail, I found this message:

GERONIMO, DEAR FRIEND,

I've read with great pleasure the article about the mammoth you published in *The Rodent's Gazette.* I found it very interesting. I'm extremely honored that you dedicated the discovery to me!

I'm almost ready for my first time-travel experiment. I would love for you to join me. I will contact you soon. Take care!

Paws von Volt

P.S. Thank you so very much for not squeaking about the yetis. It means a lot to me. By the way, my underwater lab is fabumouse.

There was also a picture of Professor von Volt's time-travel machine. I studied it closely. A dedication was engraved on its side. It read:

To my dear friend Geronimo Stilton,
a true gentlemouse
who knows
the value of friendship.
With great respect,
Paws von Volt.

Ah, friendship is truly a rare and precious thing. I'd say it's even more **precious** than the fur on top of my head!

I wondered when Professor von Volt would finish working on his time-travel machine. I was excited at the idea of traveling with him.

Yes, I know I'm not the most courageous of mice. *And I do hate traveling.* But for a chance to travel through time, I, *Geronimo Stilton*, just might make an exception. . . .

And that's a promise!

ABOUT THE AUTHOR

 Born in New Mouse City, Mouse Island, **GERONIMO STILTON** is Rattus Emeritus of Mousomorphic Literature and of Neo-Ratonic Comparative Philosophy. For the past twenty years, he has been running *The Rodent's Gazette,* New Mouse City's most widely read daily newspaper.

Stilton was awarded the Ratitzer Prize for his scoops on *The Curse of the Cheese Pyramid* and *The Search for Sunken Treasure.* He has also received the Andersen 2000 Prize for Personality of the Year. One of his bestsellers won the 2002 eBook Award for world's best ratlings' electronic book. His works have been published all over the globe.

In his spare time, Mr. Stilton collects antique cheese rinds and plays golf. But what he most enjoys is telling stories to his nephew Benjamin.

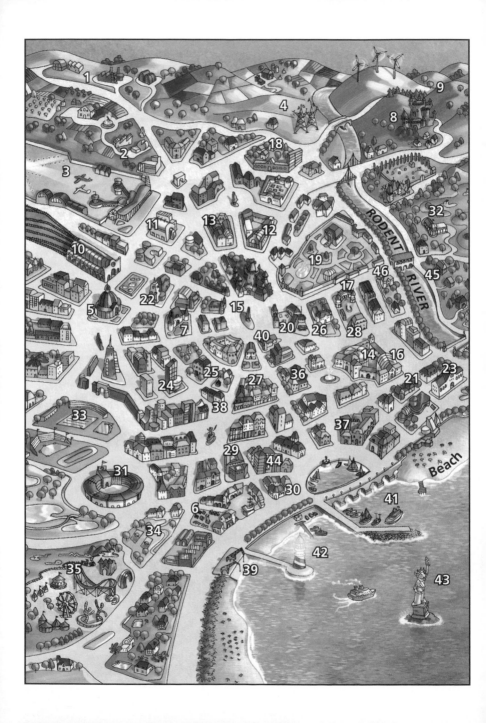

Map of New Mouse City

1. Industrial Zone
2. Cheese Factories
3. Angorat International Airport
4. WRAT Radio and Television Station
5. Cheese Market
6. Fish Market
7. Town Hall
8. Snotnose Castle
9. The Seven Hills of Mouse Island
10. Mouse Central Station
11. Trade Center
12. Movie Theater
13. Gym
14. Catnegie Hall
15. Singing Stone Plaza
16. The Gouda Theater
17. Grand Hotel
18. Mouse General Hospital
19. Botanical Gardens
20. Cheap Junk for Less (Trap's store)
21. Parking Lot
22. Mouseum of Modern Art
23. University and Library
24. *The Daily Rat*
25. *The Rodent's Gazette*
26. Trap's House
27. Fashion District
28. The Mouse House Restaurant
29. Environmental Protection Center
30. Harbor Office
31. Mousidon Square Garden
32. Golf Course
33. Swimming Pool
34. Blushing Meadow Tennis Courts
35. Curlyfur Island Amusement Park
36. Geronimo's House
37. Historic District
38. Public Library
39. Shipyard
40. Thea's House
41. New Mouse Harbor
42. Luna Lighthouse
43. The Statue of Liberty
44. Hercule Poirat's Office
45. Petunia Pretty Paws's House
46. Grandfather William's House

Don't miss any of my fabumouse adventures!

Also available in audio

www.geronimostilton.com/uk

Don't miss any of my fabumouse adventures!